NO COWHERDERS WANTED

BY

ROBERT E. HOWARD

British Library Cataloguing-in-Publication Data
A catalogue record for this book is available from the
British Library

Robert E. Howard

Robert Ervin Howard was born in Peaster, Texas in 1906. During his youth, his family moved between a variety of Texan boomtowns, and Howard – a bookish and somewhat introverted child – was steeped in the violent myths and legends of the Old South. Although he loved reading and learning, Howard developed a distinctly Texan, hardboiled outlook on the world. He became a passionate fan of boxing, taking it up at an amateur level, and from the age of nine began to write adventure tales of semi-historical bloodshed. In 1919, when Howard was thirteen, his family moved to the Central Texas hamlet of Cross Plains, where he would stay for the rest of his life.

At fifteen Howard began to read the pulp magazines of the day, and to write more seriously. The December 1922 issue of his high school newspaper featured two of his stories, 'Golden Hope Christmas' and 'West is West'. In 1924 he sold his first piece – a short caveman tale titled 'Spear and Fang' – for $16 to the not-yet-famous *Weird Tales* magazine. He published with the magazine regularly over the next few years. 1929 was a breakout year for Howard, in that the 23-year-old writer began to sell to other magazines, such as *Ghost Stories* and *Argosy*, both of whom had previously sent him hundreds of rejection slips. In 1930, he began a correspondence with weird fiction master H. P. Lovecraft which ran up to his death six years later, and is regarded as one of the great correspondence cycles in all of fantasy literature.

It was partly due to Lovecraft's encouragement that Howard created his most famous character, Conan the Cimmerian. Conan – a barbarian-turned-King during the Hyborian Age, a mythical period of some 12,000 years ago – featured in seventeen *Weird Tales* stories between 1933 and 1936, and is now regarded as having spawned the 'sword and sorcery' genre, making Howard's influence on fantasy literature comparable to that of J. R. R. Tolkien's. The Conan stories have since been adapted many times, most famously in the series of films starring Arnold Schwarzenegger.

Howard was enjoying an all-time high in sales by the beginning of 1936, but he was also deeply upset by the ill health of his mother, who had fallen into a coma. On the morning of June 11, 1936, he asked an attending nurse whether she would ever recover, and the nurse replied negatively. Howard walked to his car, parked outside the family home in Cross Plains, and shot himself. He died eight hours later, aged just thirty.

I hear a gang of buffalo hunters got together recently in a saloon in Dodge City to discuss ways and means of keeping their sculps onto their heads whilst collecting pelts, and purty soon one of 'em riz and said, "You mavericks make me sick. For the last hour you been chawin' wind about the soldiers tryin' to keep us north of the Cimarron, and belly-achin' about the Comanches, Kiowas and Apaches which yearns for our hair. You've took up all that time jawin' about sech triflin' hazards, and plannin' steps to take agen 'em, but you ain't makin' no efforts whatsoever to pertect yoreselves agen the biggest menace they is to the entire buffalo-huntin' clan--which is Breckinridge Elkins!"

That jest show's how easy prejudiced folks is. You'd think I had a grudge agen buffalo hunters, the way they takes to the bresh whenever they sees me coming. And the way they misrepresents what happened at Cordova is plumb disgustful. To hear 'em talk you'd think I was the only man there which committed any vi'lence.

If that's so I'd like to know how all them bullet holes got in the Diamond Bar saloon which I was using for a fort. Who throwed the mayor through that board fence? Who sot fire to Joe Emerson's store, jest to smoke me out? Who started the row in the first place by sticking up insulting signs in public places? They ain't no use in them fellers trying to ack innercent. Any unbiased man which was there, and survived to tell the tale, knows I acted all the way through with as much dignity as a man can ack which is being shot at by forty or fifty wild-eyed buffalo skinners.

I had never even saw a buffalo hunter before, because it was the first time I'd ever been that far East. I was taking a pasear into New Mexico with a cowpoke by the name of Glaze Bannack which I'd met in Arizona. I stopped in Albuquerque and he went on, heading for Dodge City. Well, I warn't in Albuquerque as long as I'd aimed to be, account of going broke quicker'n I expected. I had jest one dollar left after payin' for having three fellers sewed up which had somehow got afoul of my bowie knife after criticizing the Democratic party. I ain't the man to leave my opponents on the public charge.

Well, I pulled out of town and headed for the cow camps on the Pecos, aiming to git me a job. But I hadn't went far till I met a waddy riding in, and he taken a good look at me and Cap'n Kidd, and says: "You must be him. Wouldn't no other man fit the description he gimme."

"Who?" I says.

"Glaze Bannack," says he. "He gimme a letter to give to Breckinridge Elkins."

So I says, "Well, all right, gimme it." So he did, and it read as follers:

Dere Breckinridge:

I am in jail in Panther Springs for nothin all I done was kind of push the deperty sheriff with a little piece of scrap iron could I help it if he fell down and fracktured his skull Breckinridge. But they say I got to pay $Ten dolars fine and I have not got no sech money Breckinridge. But old man Garnett over on Buck Creek owes me ten bucks so you colleck from him and come and pay me out of this hencoop. The food is terrible Breckinridge. Hustle.

Yore misjedged frend.

Glaze Bannack, Eskwire.

Glaze never could stay out of trouble, not being tactful like me, but he was a purty good sort of hombre. So I headed for Buck Creek and collected the money off of Old Man Garnett, which was somewhat reluctant to give up the dough. In fact he bit me severely in the hind laig whilst I was setting on him prying his fingers loose from that there ten spot, and when I rode off down the road with the dinero, he run into his shack and got his buffalo gun and shot at me till I was clean out of sight.

But I ignored his lack of hospitality. I knowed he was too dizzy to shoot straight account of him having accidentally banged his head on a fence post which I happened to have in my hand whilst we was rassling.

I left him waving his gun and howling damnation and destruction, and I was well on the road for Panther Springs before I discovered to my disgust that my shirt was a complete rooin. I considered going back and demanding that Old Man Garnett buy me a new one, account of him being the one which tore it. But he was sech a onreasonable old cuss I decided agen it and rode on to Panther Springs, arriving there shortly after noon.

The first critter I seen was the purtiest I gal I'd saw in a coon's age. She come out of a store and stopped to talk to a young cowpuncher she called Curly. I reined Cap'n Kidd around behind a corn crib so she wouldn't see me in my scare-crow condition. After a while she went on down the street and went into a cabin with a fence around it and a front porch, which showed her folks was wealthy, and I come out from behind the crib and says to the young buck which was smirking after her and combing his hair with the other hand, I says: "Who is that there gal? The one you was jest talkin' to."

"Judith Granger," says he. "Her folks lives over to Sheba, but her old man brung her over here account of all the fellers over there was about to cut each other's throats over her. He's makin' her stay a spell with her Aunt Henrietta, which is a war-hoss if I ever seen one. The boys is so scairt of her they don't dast try to spark Judith. Except me. I persuaded the old mudhen to let me call on Judith and I'm goin' over there for supper."

"That's what you think," I says gently. "Fact is, though, Miss Granger has got a date with me."

"She didn't tell me--" he begun scowling.

"She don't know it herself, yet," I says. "But I'll tell her you was sorry you couldn't show up."

"Why, you--" he says bloodthirsty, and started for his gun, when a feller who'd been watching us from the store door, he hollered: "By golly, if it ain't Breckinridge Elkins!"

"Breckinridge Elkins?" gasped Curly, and he dropped his gun and keeled over with a low gurgle.

"Has he got a weak heart?" I ast the feller which had recognized me, and he said, "Aw, he jest fainted when he realized how clost he come to throwin' a gun on the terror of the Humbolts. Drag him over to the hoss trough, boys, and throw some water on him. Breckinridge, I owns that grocery store there, and yore paw knows me right well. As a special favor to me will you refrain from killin' anybody in my store?"

So I said all right, and then I remembered my shirt was tore too bad to call on a young lady in. I generally has 'em made to order, but they warn't time for that if I was going to eat supper with Miss Judith, so I went into the general store and bought me one. I dunno why they don't make shirts big enough to fit reasonable sized men like me. You'd think nobody but midgets wore shirts. The biggest one in the store warn't only eighteen in the collar, but I didn't figger on buttoning the collar anyway. If I'd tried to button it it would of strangled me.

So I give the feller five dollars and put it on. It fit purty clost, but I believed I could wear it if I didn't have to expand my chest or something. Of course, I had to use some of Glaze's dough to pay for it with but I didn't reckon he'd mind, considering all the trouble I was going to gitting him out of jail.

I rode down the alley behind the jail and come to a barred winder, and said, "Hey!"

Glaze looked out, kinda peaked, like his grub warn't setting well with him, but he brightened up and says, "Hurray! I been on aidge expectin' you. Go on around to the front door, Breck, and pay them coyotes the ten spot and let's go. The grub I been gitten' here would turn a lobo's stummick!"

"Well," I says, "I ain't exactly got the ten bucks, Glaze. I had to have a shirt, because mine got tore, so--"

HE GIVE A YELP LIKE a stricken elk and grabbed the bars convulsively.

"Air you crazy?" he hollered. "You squanders my money on linens and fine raiment whilst I languishes in a prison dungeon?"

"Be ca'm," I advised. "I still got five bucks of yore'n, and one of mine. All I got to do is step down to a gamblin' hall and build it up."

"Build it up!" says he fiercely. "Lissen, blast your hide! Does you know what I've had for breakfast, dinner and supper, ever since I was throwed in here? Beans! Beans! Beans!"

Here he was so overcome by emotion that he choked on the word.

"And they ain't even first-class beans, neither," he said bitterly, when he could talk again. "They're full of grit and wormholes, and I think the Mex cook washes his feet in the pot he cooks 'em in."

"Well," I says, "sech cleanliness is to be encouraged, because I never heard of one before which washed his feet in anything. Don't worry. I'll git in a poker game and win enough to pay yore fine and plenty over."

"Well, git at it," he begged. "Git me out before supper time. I wants a steak with ernyuns so bad I can smell it."

So I headed for the Golden Steer saloon.

They warn't many men in there jest then, but they was a poker game going on, and when I told 'em I craved to set in they looked me over and made room for me. They was a black whiskered cuss which said he was from Cordova which was dealing, and the first thing I noticed, was he was dealing his own hand off of the bottom of the deck. The others didn't seem to see it, but us Bear Creek folks has got eyes like hawks, otherwise we'd never live to git grown.

So I says, "I dunno what the rules is in these parts, but where I come from we almost always deals off of the top of the deck."

"Air you accusin' me of cheatin'?" he demands passionately, fumbling for his weppins and in his agitation dropping three or four extra aces out of his sleeves.

"I wouldn't think of sech a thing," I says. "Probably them marked kyards I see stickin' out of yore boot-tops is merely soovernears."

For some reason this seemed to infuriate him to the p'int of drawing a bowie knife, so I hit him over the head with a brass cuspidor and he fell under the table with a holler groan.

Some fellers run in and looked at his boots sticking out from under the table, and one of 'em said, "Hey! I'm the Justice of the Peace. You can't do that. This is a orderly town."

And another'n said, "I'm the sheriff. If you cain't keep the peace I'll have to arrest you!"

This was too much even for a mild-mannered man like me.

"Shet yore fool heads!" I roared, brandishing my fists. "I come here to pay Glaze Bannack's fine, and git him outa jail, peaceable and orderly, and I'm tryin' to raise the dough like a #$%&*! gentleman! But by golly, if you hyenas pushes me beyond endurance, I'll tear down the cussed jail and snake him out without payin' no blasted fine."

The J.P. turnt white. He says to the sheriff: "Let him alone! I've already bought these here new boots on credit on the strength of them ten bucks we gits from Bannack."

"But--" says the sheriff dubiously, and the J.P. hissed fiercely, "Shet up, you blame fool. I jest now reckernized him. That's Breckinridge Elkins!"

The sheriff turnt pale and swallered his adam's apple and says feebly, "Excuse me--I--uh--I ain't feelin' so good. I guess it's somethin' I et. I think I better ride over to the next county and git me some pills."

But I don't think he was very sick from the way he run after he got outside the saloon. If they had been a jackrabbit ahead of him he would of trompled the gizzard out of it.

Well, they taken the black whiskered gent out from under the table and started pouring water on him, and I seen it was now about supper time so I went over to the cabin where Judith lived.

I WAS MET AT THE DOOR by a iron-jawed female about the size of a ordinary barn, which give me a suspicious look and says "Well, what's you want?"

"I'm lookin' for yore sister, Miss Judith," I says, taking off my Stetson perlitely.

"What you mean, my sister?" says she with a scowl, but a much milder tone. "I'm her aunt."

"You don't mean to tell me!" I says looking plumb astonished. "Why, when I first seen you, I thought you was her herself, and couldn't figger out how nobody but a twin sister could have sech a resemblance. Well, I can see right off that youth and beauty is a family characteristic."

"Go 'long with you, you young scoundrel," says she, smirking, and giving me a nudge with her elbow which would have busted anybody's ribs but mine. "You cain't soft-soap me--come in! I'll call Judith. What's yore name?"

"Breckinridge Elkins, ma'am," I says.

"So!" says she, looking at me with new interest. "I've heard tell of you. But you got a lot more sense than they give you credit for. Oh, Judith!" she called, and the winders rattled when she let her voice go. "You got company."

Judith come in, looking purtier than ever, and when she seen me she batted her eyes and recoiled vi'lently.

"Who--who's that?" she demanded wildly.

"Mister Breckinridge Elkins, of Bear Creek, Nevader," says her aunt. "The only young man I've met in this whole dern town which has got any sense. Well, come on in and set. Supper's on the table. We was jest waitin' for Curly Jacobs," she says to me, "but if the varmint cain't git here on time, he can go hongry."

"He cain't come," I says. "He sent word by me he's sorry."

"Well, I ain't," snorted Judith's aunt. "I give him permission to jest because I figgered even a bodacious flirt like Judith wouldn't cotton to sech a sapsucker, but--"

12

"Aunt Henrietta!" protested Judith, blushing.

"I cain't abide the sight of sech weaklin's," says Aunt Henrietta, settling herself carefully into a rawhide-bottomed chair which groaned under her weight. "Drag up that bench, Breckinridge. It's the only thing in the house which has a chance of holdin' yore weight outside of the sofie in the front room. Don't argy with me, Judith! I says Curly Jacobs ain't no fit man for a gal like you. Didn't I see him strain his fool back tryin' to lift that there barrel of salt I wanted fotched to the smoke house? I finally had to tote it myself. What makes young men so blame spindlin' these days?"

"Pap blames the Republican party," I says.

"Haw! Haw! Haw!" says she in a guffaw which shook the doors on their hinges and scairt the cat into convulsions. "Young man, you got a great sense of humor. Ain't he, Judith?" says she, cracking a beef bone betwixt her teeth like it was a pecan.

Judith says yes kind of pallid, and all during the meal she eyed me kind of nervous like she was expecting me to go into a war-dance or something. Well, when we was through, and Aunt Henrietta had et enough to keep a tribe of Sioux through a hard winter, she riz up and says, "Now clear out of here whilst I washes the dishes."

"But I must help with 'em," says Judith.

Aunt Henrietta snorted. "What makes you so eager to work all of a sudden? You want yore guest to think you ain't eager for his company? Git out of here."

So she went, but I paused to say kind of doubtful to Aunt Henrietta, "I ain't shore Judith likes me much."

"Don't pay no attention to her whims," says Aunt Henrietta, picking up the water barrel to fill her dish pan. "She's a flirtatious minx. I've took a likin' to you, and if I decide yo're the right man for her, yo're as good as hitched. Nobody couldn't never do nothin' with her but me, but she's learnt who her boss is--after havin' to eat her meals off of the mantel-board a few times. Gwan in and court her and don't be backward!"

So I went on in the front room, and Judith seemed to kind of warm up to me, and ast me a lot of questions about Nevada, and finally she says she's heard me spoke of as a fighting man and hoped I ain't had no trouble in Panther Springs.

I told her no, only I had to hit one black whiskered thug from Cordova over the head with a cuspidor.

AT THAT SHE JUMPED UP like she'd sot on a pin.

"That was my uncle Jabez Granger!" she hollered. "How dast you, you big bully! You ought to be ashamed, a, great big man like you pickin' on a little feller like him which don't weigh a ounce over two hundred and fifteen pounds!"

"Aw, shucks," I said contritely. "I'm sorry Judith."

"Jest as I was beginnin' to like you," she mourned. "Now he'll write to pap and prejudice him agen you. You jest got to go and find him and apologize to him and make friends with him."

"Aw, heck," I said.

But she wouldn't listen to nothing else, so I went out and clumb onto Cap'n Kidd and went back to the Golden Steer, and when I come in everybody crawled under the tables.

"What's the matter with you all?" I says fretfully. "I'm lookin' for Jabez Granger."

"He's left for Cordova," says the barkeep, sticking his head up from behind the bar.

Well, they warn't nothing to do but foller him, so I rode by the jail and Glaze was at the winder, and he says eagerly, "Air you ready to pay me out?"

"Be patient, Glaze," I says. "I ain't got the dough yet, but I'll git it somehow as soon as I git back from Cordova."

"What?" he shrieked.

"Be ca'm like me," I advised. "You don't see me gittin' all het up, do you? I got to go catch Judith Granger's Uncle Jabez and apolergize to the old illegitimate for bustin' his conk with a spittoon. I be back tomorrer or the next day at the most."

Well, his langwidge was scandalous, considering all the trouble I was going to jest to git him out of jail, but I refused to take offense. I headed back for the Granger cabin and Judith was on the front porch.

I didn't see Aunt Henrietta, she was back in the kitchen washing dishes and singing: "They've laid Jesse James in his grave!" in a voice which loosened the shingles on the roof. So I told Judith where I was going and ast her to take some pies and cakes and things to the jail for Glaze, account of the beans was rooining his stummick, and she said she would. So I pulled stakes for Cordova.

It laid quite a ways to the east, and I figgered to catch up with Uncle Jabez before he got there, but he had a long start and was on a mighty good hoss, I reckon. Anyway, Cap'n Kidd got one of his hellfire streaks and insisted on stopping every few miles to buck all over the landscape, till I finally got sick of his muleishness and busted him over the head with my pistol. By this time we'd lost so much time I never overtaken Uncle Jabez at all and it was gitting daylight before I come in sight of Cordova.

Well, about sun-up I come onto a old feller and his wife in a ramshackle wagon drawed by a couple of skinny mules with a hound dawg. One wheel had run off into a sink hole and the mules so pore and good-for-nothing they couldn't pull it out, so I got off and laid hold on the wagon, and the old man said, "Wait a minute, young feller, whilst me and the old lady gits out to lighten the load."

"What for?" I ast. "Set still."

16

So I h'isted the wheel out, but if it had been stuck any tighter I might of had to use both hands.

"By golly!" says the old man. "I'd of swore nobody but Breckinridge Elkins could do that!"

"Well, I'm him," I says, and they both looked at me with reverence, and I ast 'em was they going to Panther Springs.

"We aim to," says the old woman, kind of hopeless. "One place is as good as another'n to old people which has been robbed out of their life's savin's."

"You all been robbed?" I ast, shocked.

"WELL," SAYS THE OLD man, "I ain't in the habit of burdenin' strangers with my woes, but as a matter of fact, we has. My name's Hopkins. I had a ranch down on the Pecos till the drouth wiped me out and we moved to Panther Springs with what little we saved from the wreck. In a ill-advised moment I started speculatin' on buffler-hides. I put in all my cash buyin' a load over on the Llano Estacado which I aimed to freight to Santa Fe and sell at a fat profit--I happen to know they're fetchin' a higher price there now than they air in Dodge City--and last night the whole blame cargo disappeared into thin air, as it were.

"We was stoppin' at Cordova for the night, and the old lady was sleepin' in the hotel and I was camped at the aidge of town with the wagon, and sometime durin' the night somebody snuck up and hit me over the head. When I come to this mornin' hides, wagon and team was all gone, and no trace. When I told the city marshal he jest laughed in my face and ast me how I'd expect him to track down a load of buffalo hides in a town which was full of 'em. Dang him! They was packed and corded neat with my old brand, the Circle A, marked on 'em in red paint.

"Joe Emerson, which owns the saloon and most all the town, taken a mortgage on our little shack in Panther Springs and loaned me enough money to buy this measly team and wagon. If we can git back to Panther Springs maybe I can git enough freightin' to do so we can kind of live, anyway."

"Well," I said, much moved by the story, "I'm goin' to Cordova, and I'll see if I cain't find yore hides."

"Thankee kindly, Breckinridge," says he. "But I got a idee them hides is already far on their way to Dodge City. Well, I hopes you has better luck in Cordova than we did."

So they driv on west and I rode east, and got to Cordova about a hour after sun-up. As I come into the aidge of town I seen a sign-board about the size of a door stuck up which says on it, in big letters, "No cowherders allowed in Cordova."

"What the hell does that mean?" I demanded wrathfully of a feller which had stopped by it to light him a cigaret. And he says, "Jest what it says! Cordova's full of buffler hunters in for a spree and they don't like cowboys. Big as you be, I'd advise you to light a shuck for somewhere else. Bull Croghan put that sign up, and you ought to seen what happened to the last puncher which ignored it!"

"#$%&*!" I says in a voice which shook the beans out of the mesquite trees for miles around. And so saying I pulled up the sign and headed for main street with it in my hand. I am as peaceful and mild-mannered a critter as you could hope to meet, but even with me a man can go too damned far. This here's a free country and no derned hairy-necked buffalo-skinner can draw boundary lines for us cowpunchers and git away with it--not whilst I can pull a trigger.

They was very few people on the street and sech as was looked at me surprized-like.

"Where the hell is them fool buffalo hunters?" I roared, and a feller says, "They're all gone to the race track east of town to race hosses, except Bull Croghan, which is takin' hisself a dram in the Diamond Bar."

So I lit and stalked into the Diamond Bar with my spurs ajingling and my disposition gitting thornier every second. They was a big hairy critter in buckskins and moccasins standing at the bar drinking whiskey and talking to the bar-keep and a flashy-dressed gent with slick hair and a diamond hoss-shoe stickpin. They all turnt and gaped at me, and the hunter reched for his belt where he was wearing the longest knife I ever seen.

"Who air you?" he gasped.

"A cowman!" I roared, brandishing the sign. "Air you Bull Croghan?"

"Yes," says he. "What about it?"

So I busted the sign-board over his head and he fell onto the floor yelling bloody murder and trying to draw his knife. The board was splintered, but the stake it had been fastened to was a purty good-sized post, so I took and beat him over the head with it till the bartender tried to shoot me with a sawed-off shotgun.

I grabbed the barrel and the charge jest busted a shelf-load of whiskey bottles and I throwed the shotgun through a nearby winder. As I neglected to git the bartender loose from it first, it appears he went along with it. Anyway, he picked hisself up off of the ground, bleeding freely, and headed east down the street shrieking, "Help! Murder! A cowboy is killin' Croghan and Emerson!"

WHICH WAS A LIE, BECAUSE Croghan had crawled out the front door on his all-fours whilst I was tending to the bar-keep, and if Emerson had showed any jedgment he wouldn't of got his sculp laid open to the bone. How did I know he was jest trying to hide behind the bar? I thought he was going for a gun he had hid back there. As soon as I realized the truth I dropped what was left of the bung starter and commenced pouring water on Emerson, and purty soon he sot up and looked around wild-eyed with blood and water dripping off of his head.

"What happened?" he gurgled.

"Nothin' to git excited about," I assured him knocking the neck off of a bottle of whiskey. "I'm lookin' for a Gent named Jabez Granger."

It was at this moment that the city marshal opened fire on me through the back door. He grazed my neck with his first slug and would probably of hit me with the next if I hadn't shot the gun out of his hand. He then run off down the alley. I pursued him and catched him when he looked back over his shoulder and hit a garbage can.

"I'm a officer of the law!" he howled, trying to git his neck out from under my foot so as he could draw his bowie. "Don't you dast assault no officer of the law."

"I ain't," I snarled, kicking the knife out of his hand, and kind of casually swiping my spur acrost his whiskers. "But a officer which lets a old man git robbed of his buffalo hides, and then laughs in his face, ain't deservin' to be no officer. Gimme that badge! I demotes you to a private citizen!"

I then hung him onto a nearby hen-roost by the seat of his britches and went back up the alley, ignoring his impassioned profanity. I didn't go in at the back door of the saloon, because I figgered Joe Emerson might be laying to shoot me as I come in. So I went around the saloon to the front and run smack onto a mob of buffalo hunters which had evidently been summoned from the race track by the bar-keep. They had Bull Croghan at the hoss trough and was trying to wash the blood off of him, and they was all yelling and cussing so loud they didn't see me at first.

"Air we to be defied in our own lair by a #$%&*! cowsheperd?" howled Croghan. "Scatter and comb the town for him! He's hidin' down some back alley, like as not. We'll hang him in front of the Diamond Bar and stick his sculp onto a pole as a warnin' to all his breed! Jest lemme lay eyes onto him again--"

"Well, all you got to do is turn around," I says. And they all whirled so quick they dropped Croghan into the hoss trough. They gaped at me with their mouths open for a second. Croghan riz out of the water snorting and spluttering, and yelled, "Well, what you waitin' on? Grab him!"

It was in trying to obey his instructions that three of 'em got their skulls fractured, and whilst the others was stumbling and falling over 'em, I backed into the saloon and pulled my six-shooters and issued a defiance to the world at large and buffalo hunters in particular.

They run for cover behind hitch racks and troughs and porches and fences, and a feller in a plug hat come out and says, "Gentlemen! Le's don't have no bloodshed within the city limits! As mayor of this fair city, I--"

It was at this instant that Croghan picked him up and throwed him through a board fence into a cabbage patch where he lay till somebody revived him a few hours later.

The hunters then all started shooting at me with .50 caliber Sharps' buffalo rifles. Emerson, which was hiding behind a Schlitz sign-board, hollered something amazing account of the holes which was being knocked in the roof and walls. The big sign in front was shot to splinters, and the mirror behind the bar was riddled, and all the bottles on the shelves and the hanging lamps was busted. It's plumb astonishing the damage a bushel or so of them big slugs can do to a saloon.

They went right through the walls. If I hadn't kept moving all the time I'd of been shot to rags, and I did git several bullets through my clothes and three or four grazed some hide off. But even so I had the aidge, because they couldn't see me only for glimpses now and then through the winders and was shooting more or less blind because I had 'em all spotted and slung lead so fast and clost they didn't dast show theirselves long enough to take good aim.

BUT MY CA'TRIDGES BEGUN to run short so I made a sally out into the alley jest as one of 'em was trying to sneak in the back door. I hear tell he is very bitter toward me about his teeth, but I like to know how he expects to git kicked in the mouth without losing some fangs.

So I jumped over his writhing carcase and run down the alley, winging three or four as I went and collecting a pistol ball in my hind laig. They was hiding behind board fences on each side of the alley but them boards wouldn't stop a .45 slug. They all shot at me, but they misjedged my speed. I move a lot faster than most folks expect.

Anyway, I was out of the alley before they could git their wits back. And as I went past the hitch rack where Cap'n Kidd was champing and snorting to git into the fight, I grabbed my Winchester .45-90 off of the saddle, and run acrost the street. The hunters which was still shooting at the front of the Diamond Bar seen me and that's when I got my spurs shot off, but I ducked into Emerson's General Store whilst the clerks all run shrieking out the back way.

As for that misguided hunter which tried to confiscate Cap'n Kidd, I ain't to blame for what happened to him. They're going around now saying I trained Cap'n Kidd special to jump onto a buffalo hunter with all four feet after kicking him through a corral fence. That's a lie. I didn't have to train him. He thought of it hisself. The idjit which tried to take him ought to be thankful he was able to walk with crutches inside of ten months.

Well, I was now on the same side of the street as the hunters was, so as soon as I started shooting at 'em from the store winders they run acrost the street and taken refuge in a dance hall right acrost from the store and started shooting back at me, and Joe Emerson hollered louder'n ever, because he owned the dance hall too. All the citizens of the town had bolted into the hills long ago, and left us to fight it out.

Well, I piled sides of pork and barrels of pickles and bolts of calico in the winders, and shot over 'em, and I built my barricades so solid even them buffalo guns couldn't shoot through 'em. They was plenty of Colt and Winchester ammunition in the store, and whiskey, so I knowed I could hold the fort indefinite.

Them hunters could tell they warn't doing no damage so purty soon I heard Croghan bellering, "Go git that cannon the soldiers loaned the folks to fight the Apaches with. It's over behind the city hall. Bring it in at the back door. We'll blast him out of his fort, by golly!"

"You'll ruin my store!" screamed Emerson.

"I'll rooin' your face if you don't shet up," opined Croghan. "Gwan!"

Well, they kept shooting and so did I and I must of hit some of 'em, jedging from the blood-curdling yells that went up from time to time. Then a most remarkable racket of cussing busted out, and from the remarks passed, I gathered that they'd brung the cannon and somehow got it stuck in the back door of the dance hall. The shooting kind of died down whilst they rassled with it and in the lull I heard me a noise out behind the store.

THEY WARN'T NO WINDERS in the back, which is why they hadn't shot at me from that direction. I snuck back and looked through a crack in the door and I seen a feller in the dry gully which run along behind the store, and he had a can of kerosine and some matches and was setting the store on fire.

I jest started to shoot when I recognized Judith Granger's Uncle Jabez. I laid down my Winchester and opened the door soft and easy and pounced out on him, but he let out a squawk and dodged and run down the gully. The shooting acrost the street broke out again, but I give no heed, because I warn't going to let him git away from me again. I run him down the gully about a hundred yards and catched him, and taken his pistol away from him, but he got hold of a rock which he hammered me on the head with till I nigh lost patience with him.

But I didn't want to injure him account of Judith, so I merely kicked him in the belly and then throwed him before he could git his breath back, and sot on him, and says, "Blast yore hide, I apolergizes for lammin' you with that there cuspidor. Does you accept my apology, you pot-bellied hoss-thief?"

"Never!" says he rampacious. "A Granger never forgits!"

So I taken him by the ears and beat his head agen a rock till he gasps, "Let up! I accepts yore apology, you #$%&*!"

"All right." I says, arising and dusting my hands, "and if you ever goes back on yore word, I'll hang yore mangy hide to the--"

It was at that moment that Emerson's General Store blew up with a ear-splitting bang.

"What the hell?" shrieked Uncle Jabez, staggering, as the air was filled with fragments of groceries and pieces of flying timbers.

"Aw," I said disgustedly, "I reckon a stray bullet hit a barrel of gunpowder. I aimed to move them barrels out of the line of fire, but kind of forgot about it--"

But Uncle Jabez had bit the dust. I hear tell he claims I hit him onexpected with a wagon pole. I didn't do no sech thing. It was a section of the porch roof which fell on him, and if he'd been watching, and ducked like I did, it wouldn't of hit him.

I clumb out of the gully and found myself opposite from the Diamond Bar. Bull Croghan and the hunters was pouring out of the dance hall whooping and yelling, and Joe Emerson was tearing his hair and howling like a timber wolf with the belly ache because his store was blowed up and his saloon was shot all to pieces.

But nobody paid no attention to him. They went surging acrost the street and nobody seen me when I crossed it from the other side and went into the alley that run behind the saloon. I run on down it till I got to the dance hall, and sure enough, the cannon was stuck in the back door. It warn't wide enough for the wheels to git through.

I HEARD CROGHAN ROARING acrost the street, "Poke into the debray, boys! Elkins' remains must be here somewheres, unless he was plumb dissolved! That--!"

Crash!

They was a splintering of planks, and somebody yelled, "Hey! Croghan's fell into a well or somethin'!"

I heard Joe Emerson shriek, "Dammitt, stay away from there! Don't--"

I tore away a section of the wall and got the cannon loose and run it up to the front door of the dance hall and looked out. Them hunters was all ganged up with their backs to the dance hall, all bent over whilst they was apparently trying to pull Croghan out of some hole he'd fell into headfirst. His cussing sounded kinda muffled. Joe Emerson was having a fit at the aidge of the crowd.

Well, they'd loaded that there cannon with nails and spikes and lead slugs and carpet tacks and sech like, but I put in a double handful of beer bottle caps jest for good measure, and touched her off. It made a noise like a thunder clap and the recoil knocked me about seventeen foot, but you should of heard the yell them hunters let out when that hurricane of scrap iron hit 'em in the seat of the britches. It was amazing!

To my disgust, though, it didn't kill none of 'em. Seems like the charge was too heavy for the powder, so all it done was knock 'em off their feet and tear the britches off of 'em.

However, it swept the ground clean of 'em like a broom, and left 'em all standing on their necks in the gully behind where the store had been, except Croghan whose feet I still perceived sticking up out of the ruins.

Before they could recover their wits, if they ever had any, I run acrost the street and started beating 'em over the head with a pillar I tore off of the saloon porch. Some sech as was able ariz and fled howling into the desert. I hear tell some of 'em didn't stop till they got to Dodge City, having run right through a Kiowa war-party and scairt them pore Injuns till they turnt white.

Well, I laid holt of Croghan's laigs and hauled him out of the place he had fell into, which seemed to be a kind of cellar which had been under the floor of the store. Croghan's conversation didn't noways make sense, and every time I let go of him he fell on his neck.

So I abandoned him in disgust and looked down into the cellar to see what was in it that Emerson should of took so much to keep it hid. Well, it was plumb full of buffalo hides, all corded into neat bundles! At that Emerson started to run, but I grabbed him, and reached down with the other hand and hauled a bundle out. It was marked with a red Circle A brand.

"So!" I says to Emerson, impulsively busting him in the snout. "You stole old man Hopkins' hides yoreself! Perjuice that mortgage! Where's the old man's wagon and team?"

"I got 'em hid in my livery stable," he moaned.

"Go hitch 'em up and bring 'em here," I says. "And if you tries to run off, I'll track you down and sculp you alive!"

I went and got Cap'n Kidd and watered him. When I got back, Emerson come up with the wagon and team, so I told him to load on them hides.

"I'm a ruined man!" sniveled he. "I ain't able to load no hides."

"The exercize'll do you good," I assured him, kicking the seat loose from his pants, so he give a harassed howl and went to work. About this time Croghan sot up and gaped at me weirdly.

"It all comes back to me!" he gurgled. "We was going to run Breckinridge Elkins out of town!"

He then fell back and went into shrieks of hysterical laughter which was most hair raising to hear.

"The wagon's loaded," panted Joe Emerson. "Take it and git out and be quick!"

"Well, let this be a lesson to you," I says, ignoring his hostile attitude. "Honesty's always the best policy!"

I then hit him over the head with a wagon spoke and clucked to the hosses and we headed for Panther Springs.

Old man Hopkins' mules had give out half way to Panther Springs. Him and the old lady was camped there when I drove up. I never seen folks so happy in my life as they was when I handed the team, wagon, hides and mortgage over to 'em. They both cried and the old lady kissed me, and the old man hugged me, and I thought I'd plumb die of embarrassment before I could git away. But I did finally, and headed for Panther Springs again, because I still had to raise the dough to git Glaze out of jail.

I GOT THERE ABOUT SUN-UP and headed straight for Judith's cabin to tell her I'd made friends with Uncle Jabez. Aunt Henrietta was cleaning a carpet on the front porch and looking mad. When I come up she stared at me and said, "Good land, Breckinridge, what happened to you?"

"Aw, nothin'," I says. "Jest a argument with them fool buffalo hunters over to Cordova. They'd cleaned a old gent and his old lady of their buffalo hides, to say nothin' of their hosses and wagon. So I rid on to see what I could do about it. Them hairy-necked hunters didn't believe me when I said I wanted them hides, so I had to persuade 'em a leetle. On'y thing is they is sayin' now that I was to blame fer the hull affair. I apologized to Judith's uncle, too. Had to chase him from here to Cordova. Where's Judith?"

"Gone!" she says, stabbing her broom at the floor so vicious she broke the handle off. "When she taken them pies and cakes to yore fool friend down to the jail house, she taken a shine to him at first sight. So she borrored the money from me to pay his fine--said she wanted a new dress to look nice in for you, the deceitful hussy! If I'd knowed what she wanted it for she wouldn't of got it--she'd of got somethin' acrost my knee! But she paid him out of the jug, and--"

"And what happened then?" I says wildly.

"She left me a note," snarled Aunt Henrietta, giving the carpet a whack that tore it into six pieces. "She said anyway she was afeared if she didn't marry him I'd make her marry you. She must of sent you off on that wild goose chase a purpose. Then she met him, and--well, they snuck out and got married and air now on their way to Denver for their honeymoon--Hey, what's the matter? Air you sick?"

"I be," I gurgled. "The ingratitude of mankind cuts me to the gizzard! After all I'd did for Glaze Bannack! Well, by golly, this is lesson to me! I bet I don't never work my fingers to the quick gittin' another ranny out of jail!"